CW00802898

# Joseph Wilderness Adventure

## A Trip to Shenandoah National Park

### Christine M. Miller

Illustrated by
Julia Robinson

**TRIPLE PEAKS PRESS**

# Copyright © 2022 by Christine M. Miller

This is a work of fiction. Names, characters, places, and incidents either are the product of the author's imagination or are used fictitiously. Any resemblance to actual persons, (living or dead), events, or locales is entirely coincidental.
All rights reserved. No portion of this book may be reproduced in any form by any electronic or mechanical means (including photocopying, recording, or information storage and retrieval) without written permission from the author, except for the use of brief quotations in a book review.

TRIPLE PEAKS PRESS PUBLISHING

FOR MORE INFORMATION AND BULK SALES, CONTACT US:
TRIPLEPEAKSPRESS@GMAIL.COM

LIBRARY OF CONGRESS CATALOGING-IN-PUBLICATION DATA
The Library of Congress has cataloged the paperback edition of this work as follows:
Names: Miller, Christine M., author
Title: Josephine's Wilderness Adventure A Trip to Shenandoah National Park / by Christine M. Miller
Description: Triple Peaks Press, [2022].
Audience: Ages 8-12, grades 3-7.
Summary: When 9-year-old Josephine learns that the family summer vacation will be a wilderness camping adventure, her fantasy world of seeking out nature comes to life.
Identifiers: LCCN 2022911631
Subjects: [1. History of Shenandoah National Park– Fiction. 2. Wilderness–Fiction. 3. Courage–Fiction. 4. Appalachian Trail– Fiction. 5. Black bears–Fiction. 6. Birds of prey–Fiction. 7. Leave No Trace principles–Fiction. 8. Nature–Fiction. 9. Character Education–Fiction. 10. Camping–Fiction.]

ISBN 979–8-218- 02529-8 (paperback)
Library of Congress Control Number 2022911631

Editor: Terri Gillespie
Cover design and book illustrations: Julia Robinson

Printed and bound in the United States of America by IngramSpark

First Edition: August 2022

*For My Parents*

# CONTENTS

1. The Secret Spot

2. Packing the Essentials

3. The Skyline Drive

4. Home Away From Home

5. Junior Ranger Program

6. The Amphitheater

7. Wild Blueberry Picking

8. Dark Hollow Falls

9. Shower House

10. "Going for a Ride"

## CHAPTER 1

# The Secret Spot

JOSEPHINE, OR JO as everyone called her, was leisurely perched twenty feet above the ground in the forked branches of an old Kousa dogwood tree. The rough bark against her skin felt earthy. The ease with which she could balance her limbs and become entwined with the old tree felt effortless.

It was here in this simple, secluded place where Jo would go to escape everything else going on in her life for hours on end. Her house was always filled with chatter from her sisters, so she liked to sneak away and be alone with her thoughts. The revolving world around Jo seemed to vanish. All that remained was the sound and feel of nature surrounding her in her own little secret spot. She watched the squirrels scamper around on the ground below. She listened to the birds singing in concert from nearby trees. She felt the warmth of the early summer sun on her darkening olive skin as it penetrated through the leaf-thick tree branches.

Jo, a cheerful 9-year-old with hidden muscular strength that developed naturally from staying active, didn't have a lot in common with girls in the neighborhood. She was, however, happy with the casual friendships she made with the boys who lived on her block. One afternoon last fall, a group of boys needed another player to even out the teams for a game of street hockey. Jo boldly offered to play. It didn't take long for the boys to realize that inside that slender-framed girl with the brown braided pigtails was a scrappy hockey player. Jo liked playing with the boys because in her mind they were less complicated than girls. Strangely, her parents approved. They seemed to think playing hockey in the street was safer than wandering off to the park.

Suddenly, Jo heard the unmistakable familiar sound of her dad's whistle echoing from a distance. Her imaginary adventure in the wilderness, which for Jo was the park down the street from her row home in the city, was once again interrupted. She quickly scrambled down, hands and arms gripping the tree bark. Her feet stepped down one branch at a time with familiar ease. The quickened thumping in her chest, along with the hurried pace of her worn-out sneakers on the pavement, were a familiar sensation.

This particular sensation always followed the distinctive high-pitched, warbling sound made by the forcible expulsion of her dad's breath through his thumb and middle finger. If she got lucky, he would be distracted by one of her four sisters. She needed enough time to return home so she wouldn't have to answer questions about where she'd been. Jo wasn't supposed to go to the park alone, but she did it anyway. Something deep inside her, like a powerful pull of an internal compass, was leading her to seek out little pockets of nature time and time again.

Jo arrived back at her row home and slipped in unnoticed by climbing down into an open basement window. Then, she emerged up into the kitchen. Here, a family meeting was about to start. Josephine's dad was an eighth-grade history teacher. He also worked night shifts as a security guard along the shipping docks in the city of Philadelphia.

His second job meant that he wasn't home a lot, but earning the extra money was the only way the family could afford to go on summer vacations. Jo always looked forward to summer because life slowed down and her family spent time together traveling in their pop-up tent camper. For as long as Jo could remember, summers were always mini living history lessons. History wasn't necessarily her favorite subject in school, but her dad was a great storyteller who made learning fun and interesting.

During July and August every year, they escaped the city heat, and her parents would take the family around the country to various historic destinations. Last summer, in 1967, they visited the settlement at Jamestown, Virginia. It was the first successful English settlement on the mainland of North America back in 1607. Jo vividly remembered the story told by the National Park Ranger of the lost colony of Roanoke. She still wondered what happened to the small group of colonists that disappeared without a trace. Some of the colonists sailed back to England for supplies, only to return and find the small group they left behind had vanished.

When Jo closed her eyes, she could transport herself back in time to that very moment and relive what it felt like. She had freely wandered around the grounds of the deserted settlement. There were grass-covered mounds of dirt beneath her and an eerie silence that settled into the bunker around where the settlement had once been. Learning adventures like this would stay with Jo and become a part of her for-ever. On more than one occasion in school, Jo was able to contribute firsthand knowledge and share her experiences from her summer adventures with her teachers and classmates.

This year's summer trip destination was about to be revealed at the impromptu family meeting. Her mom, a loving, reliable family referee, and her four sisters gathered around the well-worn kitchen table. Everyone settled into their assigned seats. The sisters not only had specific places to sit; their father also had assigned each of them a numerical "name." This playful approach to getting his daughters' attention was based on birth order, so the oldest was "number one" and so on. Josephine was known as "number four," followed by the baby, "number five." He even used this system when introducing them to other people!

The kitchen table was positioned in the corner of the room. It had two long benches that formed an L shape in the corner. Jo and her sisters always sat in their assigned places. There were also two stand-alone single chairs. Her dad always sat straight across from Jo with her mom in the other chair to her left.

Jo's dad began to explain that money was very tight this year so the family vacation would need to be adjusted accordingly. In order to stretch the funds the family had saved, they would need to pick a destination that didn't cost too much. The goal was to spend as many days away from the city heat as possible. This would mean finding inexpensive nightly camping fees, mostly free activities, and simple homemade meals for the family of seven. Jo's dad reassured everyone that he had found the perfect destination that was affordable, full of adventure, and educational.

The summer trip destination was Shenandoah National Park. It was a mountainous wilderness nestled in the beautiful Blue Ridge Mountains of Virginia. Josephine feared her insides might burst with joy right out onto the kitchen table.

"When do we leave?" she blurted out.

Then, realizing she had called out and interrupted her dad, Jo paused and waited for his reaction. His eyes locked onto hers. She wondered what kind of mood he was in today because his current stone-faced expression was unreadable. And then she saw it. The corners of his mouth turned upward ever so slightly and grew wider across his face.

"Soon, Josephine."

He added a quick wink.

"Very soon," he exclaimed.

Jo imagined his wink was invisible to everyone in the room but her. Her dad was a wizard when it came to making each daughter feel special.

A smile matching her dad's grew on Jo's face and similarly spread from ear to ear. Jo was finally going to be able to see what the real wilderness was like!

## CHAPTER 2

# Packing the Essentials

JOSEPHINE WAS FILLED with excitement for the next several days while the family prepared for the trip. She seemed to become a more responsible kid virtually overnight. Jo entered the kitchen where her mom was packing food for the trip.

"Mom, I want to help by packing my own bag," Jo announced.

Jo's mom hesitated.

Then she contemplated. "Are you sure you're ready? It's a big responsibility and you've never done it before."

Jo responded confidently, "I know I'm ready. Please give me a chance? I remember the sort of things you packed for me on past camping trips."

"Well, alright. We can give it a try," her mom conceded. "My goodness, you seem to be growing up so fast these days, Josephine!"

Jo immediately went to her bedroom. She carefully sorted through her small chest of drawers in the room she shared with "number five." Then she sat down and wrote a checklist of things to pack. She wanted to include just the right clothing items and essentials for what she imagined a trip into the wilderness would require.

After much thought, Jo packed her small backpack with the following:

- Sturdy worn-out sneakers
- Layered clothing for both warm and cold temperatures
- Favorite Huckleberry Finn-like floppy brown hat
- Hairbands and brush for her trademark braided pigtails
- Flashlight
- Notebook and pen
- Small pair of binoculars
- Favorite book, *Escape to Witch Mountain*
- Road map of the United States
- Her collection of lifelike rubber snakes, spiders, and mice

Josephine always brought her prized collection because she enjoyed alone time playing with her rubber creatures as well as periodically scaring her mom and sisters with them.

Within a few days, all the preparations had been made. The car was packed and the tent camper was hitched to the bumper. Jo was the first one in the car. Although the travel space was a bit cramped for seven humans, especially when combined with all the camping gear, she didn't mind the close quarters of the long ride ahead this time.

Jo and her small backpack settled into the driver's side half of the small rear-facing bench seat. The seat was usually hidden, but could be flipped up in the back. That's where she and "number five" would sit during family outings. The short seat and equally short backrest met at a ninety-degree angle, and neither provided much cushioning. The foot space seemed like only a thin piece of hot, ribbed sheet metal divided the dangerous spinning of the rear wheels from the soles of a passenger's shoes.

Jo waited patiently in her travel position as everyone else slowly found their way into their respective seats. Her dad got into the captain's seat behind the wheel with his trusty hot thermos of coffee wedged between the two front seats. Her mom was chief navigator with the road maps nestled on her lap as she settled into the co-pilot seat. Her three older sisters occupied the wide middle bench seat. Her youngest sister, "number five," buckled in next to her.

Jo's dad started doing head counts before pulling out because once he left "number three" at a rest stop and drove a few miles before anyone realized it.

Jo's dad said, "Count off!"

With well-practiced timing, everyone called out her number in sequence.

"Looks like we're all in the car this time. Buckle up. Here we go!" he trumpeted.

Josephine (oh, and family!) set off for the adventure in the wilderness.

## CHAPTER 3

# The Skyline Drive

THE NEARLY FIVE-HOUR trip seemed to whiz by as quickly as the cars along the highway. Josephine and her sisters always played a game that helped pass the time. They would count how many different state license plates they saw on cars as they went by. There was also a game-winning bonus. If you were the first to see a license plate from farthest away, you became the automatic winner. Because Jo's seat faced backwards, she had the advantage of seeing the license plates before everyone else. Jo had already spotted a South Dakota plate, which put her in the running to win the game. When Jo got bored, she also liked to pull out her own map and locate the roads they traveled on and the states they passed through.

After a few hours of driving, Jo's dad wanted to share some interesting facts about the spectacular ride ahead. He called out, "Can everyone hear me?"

A resounding "Yes" echoed in unison.

"How about you two in the back?"

"Loud and clear!" replied Jo.

"Great! We're approaching the drive." Jo's dad continued, "The Skyline Drive is a scenic road 105 miles long. It runs along the crest of the Blue Ridge Mountains in Shenandoah National Park. It is the only public road that passes through the park. The milepost markers help guide visitors to points of interest along the drive. There are hiking trails, scenic overlooks, and several visitor centers and campgrounds throughout the park. Keep on the lookout for the entrance!"

Jo and her family had just reached Milepost 0 in Front Royal, Virginia, where the drive begins. It wasn't until they arrived at the northern entrance that everything slowed down to a meandering pace. After passing through the ranger station at the gate, Jo saw a large welcome sign to Shenandoah National Park. She thought the rustic wooden carved sign was a beautiful work of art.

The sign reminded her of the wood carving her dad made during the last summer trip. He had found a piece of dead wood and used his pocketknife to carve their last name into it. Then he accented the carved-out letters with a permanent black marker. At each campsite, her dad used a wire to hang it from a pole. The carved sign was like their very own personal welcome sign.

"Hey, Dad!" Jo called from the back of the station wagon, "The park welcome sign looks like the one you carved!"

"It certainly does," beamed her dad. "We brought ours on the trip and you can help me hang it when we get set up at the campsite."

Happy with the thought, Jo went back to looking out the windows, eagerly watching for the wilderness ahead.

As they followed the Skyline Drive, the scenic road curved around the mountain range and soon all she could see was dense forest everywhere she looked. Jo's dad stopped for a break at an overlook. At these paved pull-off areas, visitors could stop for scenic views. Once parked, you could get out of the car safely and walk to the edge of the mountainside.

Jo walked over to the edge and gazed out at the beautiful views of the surrounding Blue Ridge Mountains. The valley was covered with multi-green checkerboard-shaped farms. Man-made stone barriers, formed with colorful large rocks, lined the edges of the overlook, protecting visitors from steep drops.

Jo stepped up onto the knee-high stone barrier to get a better view. She spread her feet and arms out wide with her fingertips reaching for the surrounding mountain peaks. Then she raised her chin toward the sky and took in a long, slow, belly-filling breath.

Just as she was exhaling the clean mountain air, her dad walked over.

"Jo, get down from there!" he said.

"But there's such a better view from up here," replied Jo.

"It may be slightly better, but it's not safe."

Her dad reached out his hand and Jo used it to keep her balance as she jumped down onto the pavement. Then he asked, "Did you know the CCC built these stone walls?"

"What's the CCC?" Jo asked.

"The CCC, or Civilian Conservation Corps, was a government relief program created following the Great Depression. It provided unemployed young men with jobs in the late 1930s. Groups of them worked and camped on this land and developed much of what eventually became Shenandoah National Park."

"Wow!" replied Jo. "That makes these stone walls pretty old."

"Yes," said her dad. "It's amazing how well they are holding up. Things were built to last back then."

Then, after everyone had enjoyed the overlook views, Jo's dad announced, "Everyone back to the car. Time to move on!" When everyone was in, he said, "OK, count off!"

Once again, with well-practiced timing, everyone called out her number in sequence.

"Great, we're all here!" he said.

With that, the scenic drive continued. As the car with camper in tow slowly climbed the steep, winding mountain passage, Jo enjoyed her rear-facing panoramic view. Looking out the back window, she saw more stone barriers lining the road. To the right was a distant view of endless mountain peaks rising up at various heights out of the valley below. Just outside the car window on the other side, the steep, rock-covered mountain walls appeared to climb straight up until they disappeared into the clouds above. Then, just around the next bend in the curving, climbing roadway, there was yet another clear view of a steep slope down.

The mountain slope was untouched wilderness, covered with towering trees, lush thick green forest undergrowth, and small plants. The forest spread all the way down to the valley below. Jo thought at times that the rugged, ever-climbing, powerful wilderness that surrounded her might just swallow her right up. But then, Jo's heart began to swell and she smiled on the inside as she absorbed the incredible beauty of nature that was wrapping its arms around her. She felt like she was "home"!

## CHAPTER 4

# Home Away From Home

AFTER A LONG DAY of somewhat tedious driving, the dependable station wagon with camper in tow finally rolled into Big Meadows. The campground was located at Milepost 51 of the Skyline Drive. The surrounding recreational area also contained the park's Harry F. Byrd Visitor Center, the wayside store, a small amphitheater, and a beautiful meadow.

As Jo's dad turned off the paved main road onto a gravel camp road, everyone became very excited to help set up camp. First came the entertaining ritual of backing the camper onto the campsite. Jo's dad and mom worked as a team. Her mom was standing outside the car at the edge of the woods toward the back of the campsite. She gave some sort of flailing hand signals that were supposed to provide direction. Meanwhile, her dad was maneuvering the steering wheel this way and that as he slowly backed the camper.

The campsites were like little postage-stamp-size plots of cleared land plopped right in the middle of the forest. As soon as her dad gave the all-clear signal, everyone was allowed to get out of the car. Next, there was steady movement with purpose.

Everyone was given jobs to help set up the family's "home away from home."

The "home away from home" consisted of the car, the pop-up tent camper with the roof raised and the canvas-covered sides pulled out, and a four-sided screen room supported by four thin aluminum poles. The screen room was positioned so it covered the picnic table where the family would eat their meals. Inside the screen room was a makeshift kitchen area. There was a very old green Coleman camping stove, several plastic wash bins, a wooden box with cooking supplies, and a few folding chairs. Needless to say, living in the woods beneath canvas walls with no running water or electric hookups was not for everyone. Jo, however, loved the rustic setting.

*I want to stay here forever!* she thought.

Jo would be perfectly happy if she never went back to living in the confines of a house in the city with cinderblock walls. Being here was Jo's fantasy world brought to life. Her daydreaming was interrupted by the resonant sound of her dad's voice.

"'Number four!'" exclaimed her dad. "I need you to go find water and fill the water jugs."

"Sure thing!" Jo responded delightedly. "I'll go fill them right away!"

Jo grabbed the brochure with the campground map and the two collapsed plastic containers. Then, she wandered off on her own little mini adventure. As she walked along the gravel road, she observed other campsites along the way. There was a small one-person tent on the ground in the middle of a site right next to hers. Jo thought it was strange to see such a small tent and no apparent car for that person to have arrived in. She continued on down the road, referring to the map for the marked location of the water source. As the road curved around the bend, she passed various other set-ups. Some had camper vans that you drive, and others had towable campers on wheels like hers.

Jo came upon a small brick building with a wooden sign out front that said "Toilets." Being curious, Jo went in the side door marked "WOMEN" to take a look around. It was definitely not fancy. There were just a few toilets separated by wooden walls that reminded her of horse stalls. Jo remembered the time she had to dig a hole with a small camp shovel because there were no toilet facilities where they camped.

"*At least I won't have to do my business in the woods*," she thought.

Given the distance she had walked from her campsite, she decided to definitely bring her flashlight if she had to use the facilities in the dark of night. This was the wilderness after all. Of course, there was always the chance she might run into a bear. She had read that lots of black bears lived in the national park. Secretly, she hoped she would get to see one!

Down a short winding stone path just past the toilet building, Jo finally came upon the fresh water filling station. There was a wooden post in the ground with a pipe bolted to it that came up from below the earth. At the top end of the pipe was a strange-looking lever with a spigot. Jo grasped the lever and pulled upwards and the water started flowing out. She quickly took the bright red cap off her container and positioned it under the flowing water. After Jo finished filling both the jugs, she capped them and shuffled back to the campsite. As she walked, she waddled a bit from side to side from the unsteady shifting of weight in the filled water jugs. She thought about how water was used much more sparingly while camping compared to living in a sticks-and-bricks house. *These two jugs should last at least a few days here at the campsite,* Jo thought. *Back home, within a few hours this same amount of water would probably go right down the drain from faucets needlessly left running by my sisters while brushing their teeth!*

By the time Jo returned from her exploration, the campsite was all set up. After a delicious meal of ham and cheese sandwiches with potato chips and fresh mountain spring water, there was enough time for the family to take a little hike down to the visitor center. Jo's dad wanted to gather information about upcoming free park activities.

## CHAPTER 5

# Junior Ranger Program

AS JO AND HER FAMILY walked along the trail that led to the Harry F. Byrd Visitor Center, Jo had her first wildlife sighting. She saw a deer right next to the hiking trail! The deer lifted its head elegantly and looked right at Jo, then casually went back to eating grass as if it wasn't scared at all. Jo and her family carefully went around the beautiful doe, giving it a wide berth.

Just a short distance up the trail, they found the visitor center. Inside was an information desk with a ranger station. The two park rangers behind the desk, Ranger Rick and Ranger Ruth, directed Jo and her family to the various displays. One had information about the Junior Ranger program. There was also a display of trail maps, books, and postcards. Behind a half wall was an interactive exhibit telling the story of Shenandoah and how it became a wilderness destination.

Jo was especially interested in the Junior Ranger program, so she asked Ranger Rick about it.

"Ranger Rick, hi, my name's Josephine but everyone calls me Jo. Can you please tell me what the Junior Ranger program is about?"

Ranger Rick said, "Hello, Jo, it's nice to meet you. It's a program allowing kids to join the National Park Service 'family' as Junior Rangers."

He picked up a workbook.

"Kids between the ages of 5 and 13 can complete a series of activities during their park visit, share their answers with a park ranger, and receive an official Junior Ranger badge. Here, take a workbook."

Jo was super excited. She took the workbook and walked over to her dad.

"Dad, can we find out about the ranger talks?" Jo asked eagerly. "I would really like to earn a Junior Ranger badge."

"We can definitely gather information about the times and locations for a few of the ranger presentations. The talks will be interesting for everyone, I'm sure," replied her dad.

They moved to the bulletin board where park information was posted and looked at the events together. They picked two interesting ranger programs. One was about birds of prey, and the other was about bugs. Jo was excited to learn about both.

Across the large open room of the visitor center, a wall of windows reached from ceiling to floor. Jo was drawn to the view. Out the window she could see nothing but meadow. It was a beautiful sight. She stood there for a long time just looking out at the lush, brown and green wide-open area. There was a maze of trails, from where people and animals had walked. The trampled grass from feet, paws, and hooves curved around throughout the thick, tall grass and small bushes.

Ranger Ruth walked over and joined Jo. As they gazed out at the meadow, Ranger Ruth asked, "Do you know about the sunset secret?"

"No. What's the sunset secret?"

Ranger Ruth explained, "Every night at dusk, just before the sun fully sets, herds of deer wander lazily throughout the meadow grazing on the grass and bushes. It's also common for black bears to come to the meadow too because they like to eat the berries that grow wild there." Then she added, "For the animals, this is their home and natural habitat, and we humans are just visitors."

Ranger Ruth turned toward Jo and their eyes met.

"Can I tell you a secret?" Jo whispered. "I'm really hoping to see a bear."

"Seeing wildlife here can be exciting. Just remember, it's really important for the safety of both the wildlife and the visitors to keep a safe distance and admire their beauty from afar," Ranger Ruth told her.

"There was a deer along the trail on my way here to the visitor center," Jo said.

"Oh?"

"Yes, it was a beautiful doe. My family moved slowly and quietly. We crossed to the opposite side of the trail so we wouldn't scare it."

"You did the right thing to walk carefully around it and not disturb it. You should never feed the wildlife either. The animals might become too accustomed to people and come to rely on the human food. If that happens, they may not be able to survive on their own in the forest. But it sounds like you are a true nature lover. I wish all our visitors were that respectful." Ranger Ruth turned and began to walk away.

"Thanks! I'll make sure to keep a safe distance and not feed any forest animals," Jo assured.

It was almost time for the birds of prey program. Jo walked back over to the ranger station where Ranger Rick was standing.

"I wanted to say thanks for the Junior Ranger book. I'm going to try hard to earn a badge," she said.

"You are more than welcome. I hope you enjoy your visit here in the park. When you are ready, come back and show me what you have learned," said Ranger Rick.

"I wanted to thank Ranger Ruth too, but I don't see her," said Jo.

"Oh, she had to go get ready for one of our park presentations, but I'll be sure to tell her when she comes back."

"Oh, OK. Thanks," replied Jo.

Jo walked away and rejoined her family.

## CHAPTER 6

# The Amphitheater

THE BIRDS OF PREY ranger presentation was about to begin, so Jo and her family hiked along the trail that led to the amphitheater. There she saw many rows of low wooden benches that curved around in a semicircle, all facing a raised wooden stage. The seats were arranged like a movie theater, with each row a little higher than the one in front of it.

Jo walked down the aisle, then stopped a few rows from the front and sat on the end of a bench. The stage was backed by a large white wall, which was also used as a backdrop for video presentations. Jo was super excited to see Ranger Ruth standing next to the stage.

On the stage next to Ranger Ruth were two wooden boxes, which contained actual birds. Ranger Ruth was wearing a broad-brimmed hat and her park ranger uniform. She had on a light green, button-up, collared shirt with a badge; forest green khaki pants; and sturdy hiking boots. She had a really thick glove on her left hand that went all the way up to her elbow.

"Welcome everyone," she said. "I'm Ranger Ruth. I've been a park ranger here in Shenandoah for over ten years. Today I will tell you about two different birds of prey. This presentation is one of my favorite talks to give because the birds I'm about to show you are fascinating creatures. I will need everyone to stay seated and be very quiet once the birds are out. They can be easily spooked, and we don't want them to be scared by any sudden movements or noises."

Ranger Ruth gave some background about the birds.

"Today, I have with me a red-tailed hawk and a barred owl. They have both been injured but were rescued. Unfortunately, due to their injuries, they can never be released into the wild again. They are called birds of prey because they hunt and eat small animals. Birds of prey have powerful curved beaks and very sharp talons or claws on their feet for grasping or killing prey. They have exceptional eyesight and hearing for finding food at a distance or during flight."

As Ranger Ruth was talking, all Jo could do was stare at that thick, heavy glove she was wearing. Finally, Ranger Ruth reached into the box and brought out a red-tailed hawk. A short leash was attached around one of the hawk's legs and the other end was wrapped a few times around the ranger's hand so the bird couldn't fly away. It was the most beautiful bird Jo had ever seen. The hawk's talons gripped the ranger's glove-covered arm and Jo finally understood why the glove was so thick. Those talons were sharp!

Jo barely remembered the rest of what the ranger said because she was mesmerized with the behavior of the hawk. It was watching everything around it. It turned its head almost all the way around in both directions as if it was listening too. At one point the hawk got startled and began flapping its wings.

*What a magnificent creature!* thought Jo.

Its broad wings, brown with dark tips, flapped, and its distinctive copper-red tail feathers fanned out. Ranger Ruth settled it down and it perched back on her arm for the remainder of the talk until she returned it to the box.

The other box contained an owl and, as Ranger Ruth brought it out to show and talk about it, she followed the same careful procedure of attaching the leash to her hand.

"This is a barred owl," she said. "Owls hunt at night and fly almost silently due to their special feather structure. They have very good hearing and nocturnal eyesight."

Ranger Ruth raised her arm, supporting the owl above her head for everyone to see.

She continued, "The best time of day to see owls is at dawn or dusk when they are most active. During the day owls mostly sleep in their resting place called a roost. When they hunt at night, they sit and wait perched up high. They scan all around for prey with their sharp eyes and ears, waiting for small animals."

Ranger Ruth lowered her arm and slowly made her way back to the box on the stage as she finished her presentation. When the birds were safely back in their boxes, the visitors were allowed to go down and talk to Ranger Ruth and ask questions.

Jo walked down to the stage and waited. When it was her turn she said, "Thanks Ranger Ruth. That was really interesting. I was wondering what kinds of animals the birds of prey eat?"

Ranger Ruth answered, "Hello again. I'm glad you came to my talk. They eat mice, squirrels, and other small rodents."

"How do the birds hunt if they live in captivity here in the park?" Jo asked.

"That's a really thoughtful question," replied Ranger Ruth. "Actually, because they are in captivity, they are fed a mixture of day-old rodents. This allows the bird to get all the nutrients it needs to stay healthy."

"Oh, that makes sense," replied Jo.

"Yes, the birds are well taken care of here."

After the talk, Jo and her family left the amphitheater and walked back to their campsite. Along the way, they chatted about the presentation, decided what they would make for dinner, and took bets on who would cook the fluffiest marshmallow over the campfire that night.

## CHAPTER 7

# Wild Blueberry Picking

THE NEXT MORNING, Josephine woke up early, before the light of day. She reached under her pillow to retrieve the clothes she had hidden there the night before. She quietly got dressed, then slowly slithered out of bed. Sensing her way in the dark through the familiar space, she tiptoed across the floor and right out the door of the camper.

Jo often woke before the rest of the family and followed this ritual of dressing and slipping outside undetected. Once, when she was only 5 years old, she wandered to a nearby campsite that had a makeshift rope swing. She climbed up one of the long ropes all the way to the top where it was tied to a tree branch. She pulled herself up onto the branch and sat up there in the dark quiet of the early morning. She watched the light change as the break of day revealed a glorious sunrise.

When her dad came outside with his morning cup of coffee and discovered Jo thirty feet up in the tree, he studied the situation for a minute. He realized he couldn't possibly climb up and save her, so he finally called to her to come down carefully. He tried to stay calm, but was visibly nervous as he helplessly watched "number four" take hold of the rope, wrap her legs around it, and shinny down like an inchworm. Jo was much older now and had learned her lesson from that incident, but she still loved the peacefulness of mornings by herself.

As Jo sat in her camp chair listening to the natural sounds of the forest, the sunlight grew brighter on the eastern horizon. The dark shadows lifted, and earthy green and brown hues of the forest became vibrant again with the dawning of a new day. Jo was daydreaming about bears and still hoping to see one when all of the sudden bloodcurdling screams started coming from inside the camper. Jo knew instantly the sounds came from "number three," who was once found standing on the toilet seat screaming because she had seen a mouse scampering around on the bathroom floor at home.

Jo heard her mom rustling about inside the camper then, sure enough, consoling "number three" as she tried to calm her back down.

Next, Jo's mom snapped, "Josephine, get in here!"

When her mom called her by her full name, it was never a good sign. Jo walked over to the camper and opened the door. Her mom was standing inside holding the end of a long tail attached to a very lifelike grey rubber mouse.

Her mom glowered. "What is this?"

It was definitely a toy mouse from Jo's prized collection.

"It must have fallen onto the floor when I got out of bed," said Jo.

She continued pleading her case.

"Honestly, I didn't see it fall on the floor! It was still dark when I left the camper," Jo lamented.

Jo successfully convinced her mom that it was an accident and she didn't intend to scare anyone. Her mom firmly handed her the toy with sound instructions.

"Put it away and keep it away for the rest of the trip!" she scolded.

Soon the rest of the family was up, and everyone went about the morning routine as if nothing had happened. They prepared breakfast and cleaned up the campsite, working quickly because they wanted to get going. Today was wild blueberry picking day in the meadow.

At midday, everyone set off along the trail leading to the meadow. Josephine skipped along happily, her Huckleberry Finn-like hat and braided hair both flopping up and down with each hop step. At last the visitor center and meadow came into view, with part of the Skyline Drive passing between them. The road was busy with cars, so Jo's mom gathered everyone together so they could cross safely.

Once they were gathered at the edge of the meadow, Jo's dad gave a mini history lesson about the national park plants before the blueberry picking began.

He said, "Shenandoah has over 1,400 species of plants. The plants in the park are protected by law and may not be disturbed or collected. This includes parts of plants too, such as flowers, seeds, leaves, branches, and roots."

An eye-twinkling, electrifying smile grew across his face.

"There are some exceptions, however," Jo's dad explained. "Ranger Rick told me that small amounts of fruit, about a quart per person, may be collected each day because that doesn't hurt the plant."

He explained that, in addition to blueberries, visitors could pick the blackberries, apples, wild grapes, walnuts, and hickory nuts that grew throughout the park.

He bent down and plucked a few ripe wild blueberries from a bush to show everyone what they looked like.

*Wild blueberries are much smaller than grocery store berries,* thought Jo.

"We can each gather a quart of blueberries!" Then he cupped his large hands together with his palms facing up. "What can fit in my two hands is about a quart," he explained.

"Here are the rules for today." Jo's dad stood up tall and pointed his finger down the line at each daughter as he spoke. "I want everyone to stick to blueberry picking only. You need to stay in the meadow. Don't go near the road. Don't eat the berries until they are checked, and come back when you hear my whistle."

Jo wandered off into the meadow alone searching for the small wild blueberry bushes her dad had shown her. When she came upon a bush, thick with tiny ripe berries, she realized she needed something to collect them in. She took off her floppy hat and figured the inside of it was about the size of her dad's cupped hands, so she decided to use it to collect her sweet treasures.

Down on her hands and knees, she crawled around reaching for each small berry. She gently plucked them from the thin, delicate branches and placed them into her hat.

As the warm sun rose higher in the sky, Jo's hat filled up. She tried to ignore the beads of sweat forming on her unprotected forehead. Her focus, in fact, became smaller and smaller. Soon, her eyes only saw the branch of the bush directly in front of her. Just as she was about to reach for another berry, she saw something move on the ground near her knee. As she turned her head to look, she felt her body go completely stiff. She was eye to eye with a huge snake!

"Eek!" Jo cried out.

She jumped to her feet, nearly spilling her hat full of berries. The snake must have been just as scared, because it spun around quickly and slithered in the opposite direction.

Jo's loud shriek alarmed her dad, who was picking not too far away. His long strides closed the gap between them in seconds as he came to her rescue.

"What's wrong?" he asked as he caught his breath.

"I saw a snake!" Jo exclaimed.

As she explained what happened, her muscles began to soften from their frozen state. Her breathing steadied and her heart, which felt like it was temporarily outside her chest, returned to a normal beat inside her ribcage. Jo realized, at that very moment, she liked nature and loved seeing wildlife at a distance, but she did not like to see it up close. Especially when she came eye to eye with a real snake unexpectedly!

Needless to say, Jo was done with blueberry picking for the day. She was ready to go back to the campsite for a relaxing dinner. Jo's dad gathered everyone back together and they followed the trail back to their "home away from home." Her mom was going to make blueberry pancakes with the freshly picked, sweet wild blueberries.

*These pancakes will taste especially good after nearly risking my life to collect all those berries!* Jo thought.

## CHAPTER 8

# Dark Hollow Falls

THE NEXT DAY, Jo sat by the campfire in her kid-size, webbed camping chair. She had just returned from Ranger Rick's morning presentation on bugs found in the park. It was a lot of fun, especially since only Jo and her dad went. They got to see bugs up close by looking through a magnifying glass as Ranger Rick passed around clear plastic boxes each displaying a different creepy-crawly critter. Jo's favorite was the centipede because it had a long, thin body with many pairs of tiny legs all along its sides. When she was holding the box, it moved with a rapid wave of leg movement and curled up into a circle. After the talk, Ranger Rick had released all the bugs back into the wild unharmed.

Jo spent the rest of the afternoon in her chair anxiously waiting for the family's night hike down to Dark Hollow Falls to begin. As she waited, she thought about the talk she had that morning with Ranger Rick about bears. Jo learned that black bears live across the continent from Canada down to Mexico. Although there are also other kinds of bears, only black bears live in Shenandoah National Park.

Ranger Rick explained that the bear population was nearly eliminated back in the early 1900s. The habitat destruction and hunting by settlers from Europe had caused the bear population to decline. Not only did the settlers cut down most of the trees for logging, they also hunted and killed bears excessively. Once the National Park lands were established in 1937, protection was offered and the black bear population began to grow again. The forest and streams in the area created ideal conditions for black bears to live. Now, once again, hundreds of black bears roamed throughout the park.

Ranger Rick told Jo that bears are most active at dawn and dusk, but are also seen by park visitors during daylight hours. He also said it was important to keep your distance from bears, not to feed any wild-life in the park, and to properly store and dispose of your food and trash. Jo had reas-sured Ranger Rick that her family wanted to enjoy the bears and wildlife safely. She told him how the family's food was kept in the car and trash was taken to the bear-proof dumpsters. Ranger Rick was im-pressed with how responsible Jo was for such a young person. He had praised her for learning about the park safety rules and following the rules so respectfully. Jo felt a warm sense of pride inside as she thought about the conversation.

As darkness set in, Jo tied the laces of her trusty worn-out sneakers and prepared for the night hike. She still held onto a secret wish. She hoped to be lucky (or unlucky) enough to see a real bear! She decided to be on the lookout both day and night for the remainder of her trip. But, as the days passed by, the chances of seeing a black bear during her visit became less and less likely.

Finally, it was time for the night hike. Jo's dad used a long stick to move the logs apart in the fire ring. Then, he poured water on the remaining hot coals of the fire to extinguish it fully. All seven family members were ready. They each carried their very own flashlight as they hiked away from camp along the darkening trail. Stars filled the sky and the moon was rising.

*The stars look so much brighter and closer up here in the mountains than they do at home. I feel like if I reached up, I could touch one!* Jo thought.

As they followed the trail, Jo was out in front, leading the way. She could see much of the path lit up by the natural glow of the moonlight. Jo didn't see any need to use her flashlight, but "number three" was whining at her from behind. Her sister was scared and wanted Jo to shine the flashlight up ahead so she could see what was coming. "Number three" held her dad's hand tightly and walked slowly along the trail.

Eventually, Jo and her family arrived at the Dark Hollow Falls parking lot, where Ranger Ruth was waiting near the sign at the trailhead. As the group of visitors gathered, Ranger Ruth explained what everyone should be prepared for during the hike.

She said, "Welcome everyone. Tonight, we will be hiking down to Dark Hollow Falls. Your vision adjusts to the darkness, so please don't use your flashlights once we get started. The white light they make when you turn them on and off makes it more difficult for your eyes to see in the dark."

Jo turned to "number three" and gave her a slight smirk as if to say *I told you so!*

Ranger Ruth continued, "Unnatural light is also disruptive to wild animal behavior, and dark night skies allow animals to thrive and survive. People can help reduce light pollution by not turning on unnecessary lights both here and at home. There's a handy trick we use to solve the problem of the white light from flashlights."

Then, Ranger Ruth handed out red squares of cellophane and rubber bands and told everyone to cover the lit end of the flashlights.

She instructed, "There is an exception to the no-flashlights rule. Only use the red glow of the covered flashlights when told to or for emergencies while we're hiking."

Ranger Ruth waved her hand and motioned for the group to move toward her onto the trail.

"It's also very important to hike carefully along the trail and to stay together as a group," she said.

With the visitors now at the entrance to the forest, Ranger Ruth shared information about nocturnal animals that live in the area.

She said, "If you look closely into the darkened forest, you might see glowing eyes from night animals staring back and watching you. Some eyes to watch for belong to owls, bats, raccoons, skunks, opossum, bobcats, and wolves."

Finally, the group set off down the steep trail toward the waterfalls. Jo positioned herself right behind Ranger Ruth so she wouldn't miss any of the interesting information she might share. As they hiked, the rocky, rough terrain of the trail slowed everyone's movement down to a snail's pace. Everyone was super focused on the placement of each and every footstep because it was much more difficult to see where you were going in the dark.

The trail was narrow, and along the edges there were spots where the ground dropped straight down the steep mountainside. You would most likely be killed if you fell over the side. As they hiked down the carved-out passage through the deep,

0# CHRISTINE M. MILLER

dark forest, Jo shifted her focus repeatedly from the trees to the uneven surface of the earth. She was intent on spotting glowing eyes of an animal, while maintaining her balance along the trail.

Meanwhile "number three," who was already afraid of the dark, was barely able to move her body in a forward direction. She had become stiff legged ever since Ranger Ruth said to watch for glowing eyes in the forest. "Number three" was so distracted that she didn't see the tree root sticking up in the middle of the trail. She tripped over it, lost her balance, and fell forward onto her hands and knees. She started crying and her whole body began shaking like she was having a convulsion of some sort. Although she had scraped her knee, she wasn't really hurt very badly. After making a big scene and holding up the hike, "number three" would be better off at the campsite, Jo's mom decided. She and her daughter headed back.

The hike continued for the rest of the group. Jo, her dad, and remaining sisters walked down, down, down as the trail curved back and forth into the hollow. The forest became even darker as the tall trees blocked the moonlight reflections. Jo could feel the temperature change too, as the cool damp air chilled her skin and settled in heavy around her.

Jo began to hear the roar of rushing water and she knew they were almost to the waterfalls. Sure enough, just around the next bend, Dark Hollow Falls came into full view. It was a glorious sight. There were beautiful cascading ripples of water rushing over the wall of the mountain down onto the rock bed and stream below. The water twinkled with a white glow where the moonlight peeked through the tree branches. Thousands of cold, misty droplets danced on the rocks and filled the air with movement.

Jo wandered over to the edge of the stream at the base of the falls. She sat down on a large rock and took off her sneakers. She dipped her feet into the cool flowing water. Then, she closed her eyes and listened to the symphony of nature's music welcoming her. *This is magical!* thought Jo.

Soon, it was time to start back and make their way up the mountain trail to the parking lot. Jo searched the trees for glowing eyes the entire way but didn't see any. Ranger Ruth saw her looking.

"The night creatures are out there, but they keep their distance due to the threat of us humans," said Ranger Ruth.

"I guess we must be pretty scary to them. I'm going to keep looking anyway," said Jo.

The climb was even slower and harder hiking the trail in reverse, but everyone made it back safely. Jo's summer trip was almost over.

As Jo lay snuggled in her bed that night, she drifted off to sleep still thinking about black bears. *Oh, how exciting it would be to see a real bear!* she thought.

## CHAPTER 9

# Shower House

THE FOLLOWING MORNING was a shower day for everyone. Jo's mom walked the girls to the shower house. The three older sisters were allowed to go in by themselves. Jo and "number five" stayed with their mom. Jo carried her own shower bag containing a towel, clean clothes, a small coin case, and her personal toiletries bag—a little zippered cloth case.

Each girl had one. They were perfect for keeping shower things organized, and their mom kept the cases stocked with toothpaste, a toothbrush, soap, and shampoo. The cases were a Christmas present from a wealthy doctor's wife who lived in the row home next door. Each sister's name was embroidered on top of her case, making it easy to grab the right one on shower day.

As Jo approached the building, she noticed that one of the five wooden doors on the single-story brick building was open. She could see inside and determined that behind each door were individual tiny shower rooms. Jo saw two girls standing outside the open door and could not stop staring. There was something interestingly odd about them.

Both had dried dirt on their faces and legs. Their hair looked like straggly rat's nests gathered into messy knots on top of their heads. Each wore a rolled-up, sweaty bandanna tied around her forehead. Jo actually had to take a step backwards as she gawked because the gagging smell of "stinky feet" coming off of their worn, threadbare clothes was so pungent.

The girls looked older than Jo's big sisters but younger than her mom. Each one carried a large metal-framed pack on her back. The packs looked heavy, based on the way they slid them off one arm at a time and transferred them to the ground with a thud.

Jo thought she recognized the rolled-up tent strapped to the base of the one girl's pack as the same small tent that had been on the campsite next to her own.

Jo was curious so she asked, "Why are you carrying a tent and such large backpacks?"

The girl with the tent explained, "We're hikers. We started walking in Georgia and hiked all the way here to Shenandoah."

Jo's mind was spinning, trying to understand. *They were walking?* She knew where Georgia was on her map, and it was many miles away—a long trip, even by car.

Sensing Jo's confusion, the girl with the tent continued, "We are attempting to 'Thru Hike' the Appalachian Trail all the way from Georgia to Maine."

"A 'Thru Hike'?" questioned Jo.

"Yes," said the hiker. "The Appalachian Trail is the longest hiking-only footpath in the world. It is roughly 2,190 miles long. The trail goes from the southern terminus near Springer Mountain, Georgia, northward through fourteen states up to the northern terminus at Katahdin, Maine. It can take about five or six months to complete the entire distance all at one time. It's called a 'Thru-Hike' when a hiker completes it within a calendar year. We're hoping to fin-ish within five months."

The second hiker shared, "We carry everything we need to survive in the wilderness in our backpacks. We have a tent, sleeping bags, food, water, and a few other essentials. Last night we slept in our tent here at Big Meadows. Every few days we shower and restock our food and water somewhere along the trail. In fact, we're going to stop at the wayside store to shop before we continue our hike north."

Jo chimed in, "That's why there was a tent with no vehicle on the campsite next to us. You are hikers!"

The girl with the tent exhaled, "Yes, but we have a small problem. The showers are coin operated, and we don't have any quarters."

Jo realized she could solve their problem.

Eager to help, she gushed, "I have plenty of quarters! You can have some of mine." Reaching into her case, she fished out four quarters and handed each of them two. Although one quarter was all that was needed to provide a five-minute timed shower, Jo decided they might need double that to actually scrub off all the trail dirt.

The girls thanked Jo and told her that they would never forget her gift of "Trail Magic." Trail Magic was the term for unexpected acts of generosity. It originated on the Appalachian Trail as people showed random acts of kindness and helped hikers who were passing through. The gifts often included drinks, food (Fritos corn chips and Snickers candy bars are favorites!), or other tokens of help to backpackers such as a free place to stay or a safe ride into town.

The girls were so grateful for the coins that in return they wanted to give something to Jo. After talking with her for a few more minutes and hearing about her night hike to Dark Hollow Falls, the girls had an idea. Since trail names were popular among hikers and typically given to fellow hikers based on some connection to a hiking experience, the girls bestowed a trail name upon Jo. They named her "Moon Dance" because of her bravery hiking in the dark with only the light of the moon to guide her way on the Dark Hollow Falls trail.

The story these two hikers shared about traveling on foot along the Appalachian Trail from Georgia to Maine was definitely an experience, one Jo had never known about. She thought it was fascinating these two girls just went off into the woods following a hiking trail for days and weeks on end. *They must have read books or done some planning for a hike like that,* she thought.

Jo said goodbye to the hikers and continued on with her shower and her day. That chance encounter really stuck with Jo. It inspired her, and she vowed to learn more about backpacking when she got home. She certainly had lots of stories from her trip to tell her teachers and friends when the new school year came around. This one for sure was going to be shared. *I even have a trail name! Moon Dance!*

Jo, her sisters, and her mom returned to their "home away from home" after their showers and hung their towels out to dry. Everyone enjoyed another delicious breakfast of blueberry pancakes and Tang. Jo thought Tang was the coolest drink ever because the astronauts in outer space drink it too. She loved to sprinkle the Vitamin C-rich powder into a jug of water and watch it turn orange as she shook it up.

After breakfast, they all worked together to clean the dishes and straighten up the campsite. Jo volunteered for trash detail. Her job was to walk around the campsite and pick up anything that didn't belong there. She was working on one of the last requirements for earning her Junior

Ranger badge. Practicing "Leave No Trace" and picking up trash was an important one. Jo had read that everyone should leave the land as they found it, or better.

Actually, Jo thought anyone could do that, no matter where you are. You could be in the wilderness or at your local park, but picking up trash was a good way to help keep nature beautiful. Her Junior Ranger activity book showed a list of the seven principles of Leave No Trace.

Leave No Trace

1. <u>Know Before You Go:</u> Know the rules for where you're going and what to bring with you.

2. <u>Choose the Right Path:</u> Stay on the trail while hiking to reduce damage.

3. <u>Trash Your Trash:</u> Take your trash with you when you leave natural areas.

4. <u>Leave What You Find:</u> Leave plants, rocks, and artifacts for others to enjoy.

5. <u>Be Careful With Fire:</u> Fires in Shenandoah are only allowed in permanent, Park-made fire rings.

6. <u>Respect Wildlife:</u> Protect wildlife by not feeding animals and by storing food properly.

7. <u>Be Kind to Other Visitors:</u> Respect visitors and their experiences in nature.

Jo finished picking up little bits of trash she found on the campsite—a plastic bread tie and a few soggy pieces of potato chips. After putting them in the trash, she washed her hands and spent the rest of the afternoon relaxing in her camp chair and reading her favorite book next to the fire.

That evening, as Jo's mom started to prepare dinner, she made an announcement.

"Tonight, we are making hot dogs and each of you is going to help cook."

This was an all-time favorite because, according to Jo, nothing tasted better than a hot dog cooked over the campfire. Jo's mom pushed hot dogs sideways onto the end of long metal cooking forks and handed them out, one by one.

"Now be careful not to get burnt, and cook them all the way through." Jo's mom instructed.

Then she returned to the screen room to heat up a large pot of baked beans on the camp stove.

Jo's dad sat relaxed in his webbed camp chair supervising the campfire cooking. With everyone gathered around he sang out, "Beans! Beans! The musical fruit! The more you eat! The more you toot! The more you toot! The better your feel! So eat your beans at every meal!"

"Oh, dad, not that silly song again!" said Jo.

"Why not? Don't you like my song, Jo? It's funny."

Jo laughed, "It's not going to be very funny when we're all in the camper later. I'm definitely unzipping part of the canvas wall to let in fresh air tonight!"

Jo refocused on her task at hand. She held her cooking fork high above the flames and flipped the hot dog over and over until it was charred and sizzling. When it looked like it was fully cooked, she put it into a long bun and squirted mustard on top. She smiled as she added a heaping spoonful of baked beans to her plate. It was a delicious end to another adventurous day. She wondered what kind of adventure tomorrow would bring.

## CHAPTER 10

# "Going for a Ride"

THE NEXT MORNING, Jo's dad and mom announced the family was "going for a ride" in the station wagon along the Skyline Drive. They took rides quite a bit on the weekends back home. Except for the gas, it was basically a low-cost activity. There was never really a destination, so they simply called it "going for a ride."

Every once in a while it became exciting, like the time they stopped at a cookie baking facility. The factory had a small store in the front of the building where they sold boxes of broken cookies for half-price. Jo remembered when her dad came out with a box the size of a small suitcase full of broken, buttery shortbread cookies in all kinds of shapes like rectangles and circles with a hole in the middle. Jo especially liked the ones with clear sugar sprinkles on top made in the shape of a pretzel.

Jo's dad found interesting places like the bakery every once in a while, which made "going for a ride" randomly interesting enough that nobody complained about it. Today's ride along the scenic Skyline Drive was definitely NOT one Jo was going to mind.

They pulled out of the campsite and drove along the gravel road, passed the parking lot of the Byrd Visitor Center, then turned left onto the Skyline Drive. The scenic road usually had some light traffic but never the amount that would cause a backup of cars. Most people were sightseeing, so if they stopped it was in the overlook parking areas. Jo was confused when her dad brought the car to a stop so soon, right in the middle of the road.

Jo looked out the side window to see what was causing the delay. There were about four cars stopped ahead in their lane and several more in the distance in the oncoming lane. Jo could see some people were out of their cars and appeared to be looking at something. Jo scanned the scene and realized there were two black bear cubs on the side of the road.

"Look! Baby bears!" Jo shouted.

At first she was excited to finally see a bear, but her excitement instantly turned to fear. As she scanned the scene more fully, she cried, "Oh no! Momma Bear is over on the other side of the road!"

She saw people with cameras outside of their cars taking pictures of the bear cubs. They had their backs to the large black bear. Jo feared for both the safety of the bears and the visitors, who were creating a terribly dangerous situation. Not only were black bears powerfully strong wild animals with sharp claws and teeth, but the mother bears also could become extremely ferocious when they were separated from their cubs. Jo frantically tried to think of what could be done to help. She thought of yelling out her window for the people to return to their cars, but they probably wouldn't be able to hear her. Her parents just sat there looking on.

Jo's thoughts screamed in her head. *This is not the zoo! This is the wilderness! These bears live here! This is not safe!*

A sick feeling rose from the pit of Jo's stomach, then her whole body felt like a shock wave of electricity was coursing through her veins.

Jo's next series of movements happened so fast it was all a blur. Her hand grasped the handle on the car door and opened it. Her worn-out sneakers hit the pavement running full tilt back in the direction of the visitor center. She ran as if her life depended on it across the grassy lawn, up the hill, and into the back entrance of the building. She burst through the door and quickly spotted Ranger Rick behind the counter.

"Ranger Rick, you need to come quick!" she pleaded.

He could sense the urgency from Jo's quivering voice and the look of panic on her face.

"Bears! Danger!" she cried.

Upon hearing this, Ranger Rick moved quickly. He grabbed keys to the pickup truck, then Jo's hand, and led her out to the truck. They both got in and Ranger Rick quickly brought the engine to a roar.

"Put on your seatbelt." Ranger Rick instructed. Then he asked, "Where's the trouble?"

Jo could barely find the words to explain the scene just up the road, so she pointed in the direction of where the bears were. "That way! Hurry!"

As the truck reached the scene, Ranger Rick saw the bear cubs, and the visitors were still taking pictures. He spoke with authority into a handheld microphone that amplified his voice outside of the truck.

"Everyone return to your vehicles immediately!" he said.

Jo held her breath as she watched both the bear cubs and Momma Bear's behavior as people followed Ranger Rick's orders and slowly returned to their cars. On the side of the road near the forest the bear cubs were frolicking in the grass. They rolled and tumbled together as they played. On the opposite side, near the meadow, Momma Bear had been pacing back and forth nervously during all the commotion.

Using the PA system once again, Ranger Rick announced, "Now everyone stay in your vehicles with the windows up. Please, remain as still as possible and do not move your vehicle!"

Jo exhaled after what felt like forever. Momma Bear moved slowly, as she cautiously crossed the road, swaying her head from side to side and watching for danger as she passed the stopped cars. *Finally*, she was reunited with her cubs. Momma Bear sniffed them up and down and used her huge right paw to pull them closer as she checked them over. Seeming satisfied after giving the bear cubs a full inspection, she used her nose to nudge their hindquarters, directing them up a hill into the safety of the trees at the edge of the forest.

Ranger Rick gave the all clear. The visitors began to disperse, driving off down the road. After the area was secure, Ranger Rick took Jo back to the visitor center, where she met up with her parents. Ranger Rick commended Jo for her brave actions and told her parents they were very lucky to have such an incredibly smart, quick-thinking daughter.

Back inside the building, Ranger Rick joined Ranger Ruth and together they presented Jo with a Junior Ranger badge. Jo beamed with pride. She looked down at the badge Ranger Ruth had pinned to her shirt and smiled with her whole body.

*I really did it! I earned a Junior Ranger badge! Wait until the kids at home see this!*

She thanked both the park rangers for teaching her so much about Shenandoah

National Park. Now all Jo wanted to do was share what she had learned about respecting wildlife and the land to help others learn to enjoy and appreciate it too.

A few days later Jo was back home in her "secret spot." She sat perched in the old tree at the park down the street from her row home. She was thinking about the amazing wilderness adventure she had with her family on the summer trip.

As she sat in that familiar tree, surrounded again by the beauty of nature right in her own neighborhood, she realized she learned an important lesson that summer. Jo noticed she was once again feeling "home" with the same sense of joy she felt out in the wilderness. She realized the feeling of "home" wasn't based on a particular location on a map. "Home" was a feeling she carried within her.

Josephine learned that no matter where you are, in the city or the wilderness, nature is right outside your door. All you have to do to is step outside and let the wonders of Mother Nature work their magic.

**The End**

# Reading Activities

PRE-READING ACTIVITY

This book is about a trip into the wilderness. Ask the students to name one thing they think would be important to pack for a trip like this. Make a list of all the suggestions. Have a class discussion about why these items are important. Challenge the students to choose only ten items that would fit into a small backpack. Allow the students to debate which ten items from the list should be packed and why.

POST-READING ACTIVITY

After reading the story, revisit the list of ten items the class decided upon. How did Jo's list compare to the class list? Were all Jo's items essential? Why do you think Jo chose to pack each of the ten items she decided on?

# Writing Activities

## WRITING SAMPLE ACTIVITY

Read the following prompts and choose one to write about. (150 words)

Prompt #1

Have you ever had an experience that you will remember for the rest of your life? Write about it and tell why it stands out as a memory that will stay with you.

Prompt #2

Do you have a special place you go to be alone? Describe your special place. What do you do there and/or what do you think about while you are there?

Prompt #3

Write about an experience you had in nature or a short story about what you imagine an experience in nature would be like.

# Discussion Topics

1. Where would you choose to go if you could go on an adventure like Josephine's? Discuss where and why. (History, Geography)

2. In the story Josephine writes down a list of things she considers important to bring and packs them in her small backpack. Why do you think she chooses each of these items? What would you want to bring in your backpack for a trip? Do you have any special possessions that you

think would be on your list? (Self-Iden-tity)

3. In the story Jo refers to "home" when she is in various locations throughout her adventures: up in a tree, in her house, at her campsite, and when in nature. What does "home" mean to Jo? What makes a place "home" to you? (Family, Belonging, Love, Nature)

4. When Josephine encounters the hikers, they say they are hiking from Georgia to Maine. How do you think Josephine knew where those states were? Can you find them on a map? What other aspects of geography are in the story? (Geography, Landscapes, Map Reading)

5. Do you think Josephine was telling the truth about the mouse on the floor of the camper being an accident? Have you ever

told a fib so you wouldn't get in trouble? Have you ever had someone not believe you when you were telling the truth? (Honesty, Character Education)

6. Outside the shower house Josephine and the hikers exchange gifts. How are the gifts the same? How are they different? Why do you think they chose the gifts they each gave? How was Josephine's gift more than just money? (Kindness, Character Education)

7. Read the seven principles of Leave No Trace (LNT) from Chapter 9. Why are these LNT principles important for the environment? Find examples in the story of when these principles were followed. List and/or discuss.

(Environmental Education)

8.  In the last chapter of the story, Josephine puts herself in possible danger. What do you think of her decision to get out of the car and run to get the ranger? What would you have done? Could Josephine have handled the situation better? How?

    Note to reader: The year was 1968 and there were no cell phones invented yet. Think about that when you answer the question. (Courage)

# Glossary

**A.T. (Appalachian Trail)** – an approximately 2,190-mile-long public footpath that traverses the Appalachian Mountains in the Eastern United States

**Birds of prey** – predatory birds, distinguished by a hooked bill and sharp talons

**Captivity** – being kept in place (such as a prison or cage) and not being able to leave or be free

**Cascading** – water pouring down rapidly and in large quantities

**CCC (Civilian Conservation Corps)** – a work relief program that gave millions of young men employment on environmental projects during the Great Depression

**Dusk** – the time of evening when it is beginning to get dark

**Emerged** – came out into view

**Habitat** – the natural home or environment of an animal

**Leave No Trace (LNT)** – these seven principles of Leave No Trace provide an easily understood framework of minimum impact practices for anyone visiting the outdoors

**Meadow** – low-lying land that is covered or mostly covered with grass

**National park** – a scenic or historically important area of countryside protected by the federal government for the enjoyment of the general public or the preservation of wildlife

**Overlook** – a commanding position or view

**Pop-up tent camper** – a type of towed recreational vehicle with collapsible roof and walls for easy storage and transport

**Ranger station** – a small building where a ranger (someone whose job is to protect a national park or forest) is based and where visitors can go for help

**Terminus** – a final goal, a finishing point

**Visitor center** – tourist information center

**Wide berth** – to avoid or stay away from

**Wilderness** – undisturbed wild natural areas

# ABOUT THE AUTHOR

Christine (trail name Moon Dance), a true nature girl at her core, has been exploring changing landscapes nearly her entire life, starting with her first camping trip at 11 months old. Passion for the great outdoors continued to be woven into life's journey as she raised three children with nature and exploration as a family core curriculum. As a retired teacher of thirty years, with a master's degree in educational leadership, she continues to impart the solace and freedom nature provides. Christine currently lives a nomadic lifestyle, traveling with her pug Roxie in an Airstream campervan. She lives simply with a very small footprint and promotes preservation of our public lands.

Lightning Source UK Ltd.
Milton Keynes UK
UKHW010756150822
407319UK00002B/589